HOW A SMALL FELLOW SOLVED A BIG PROBLEM

Jack and The Beanstalk

RETOLD AND ILLUSTRATED

by Albert Lorenz
with Joy Schleh

HARRY N. ABRAMS, INC., PUBLISHERS

Once upon a time, a poor woman lived with her only son, Jack. Their humble cottage and a cow were their only possessions. One morning the cow did not give milk.

"Jack, you must take the cow and sell her," said his mother. So Jack harnessed the cow and set off to town. Along the way, he met a man.

"Good day! Where are you going this morning?" asked the man.

"I am going to town to sell my cow," Jack answered.

"I would be very happy to buy your cow and save you the trip," said the man.

"How much will you give me?" asked Jack.

"I will give you these," said the man, holding out his hand.

"Beans? Beans for my cow?" questioned Jack.

"Not just any old beans. Magic beans," whispered the man.

"Magic beans! I'll take them," said Jack.

So the man walked away with the cow, and Jack ran all the way home with the magic beans.

"Mother! Look at what I got for the cow!" exclaimed Jack. "Magic beans!"

"Magic beans? What is their magic?" asked his mother. Jack scratched his head. He did not know.

"Beans for our cow? Jack, how could you do such a foolish thing?" cried his mother.

She took the beans, threw them out the window, and sent Jack to bed.

The next morning when Jack awoke, his room was filled with large green leaves. The leaves had sprouted from a gigantic beanstalk that was growing right outside his window. It reached up into the sky as far as Jack could see.

"They *were* magic beans!" whooped Jack. He immediately began to climb the beanstalk.

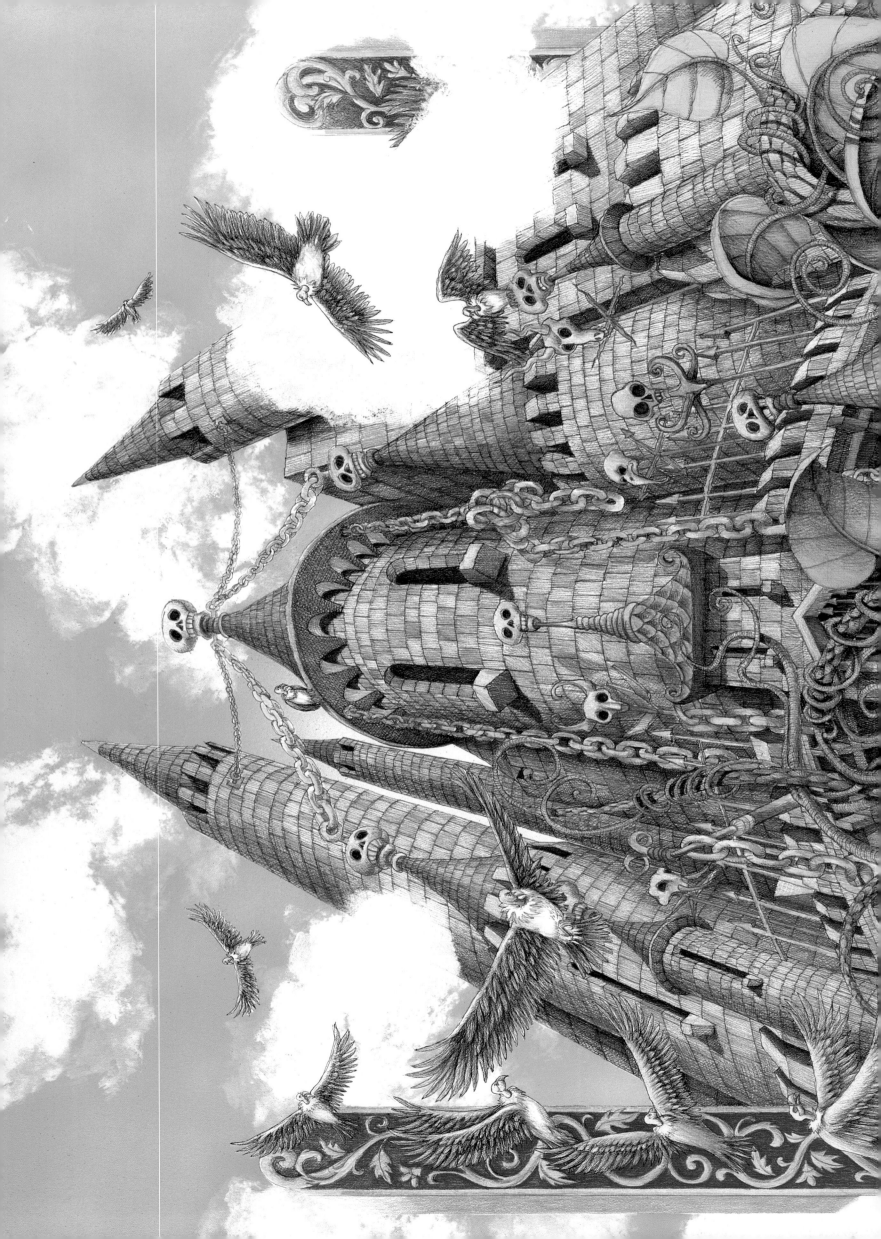

Jack climbed and climbed up through the clouds until he reached a gigantic castle.

(CAN YOU FIND HIM?)

Outside the castle door stood an enormous woman.

"Good morning," said Jack. "I'm so hungry. Could you spare me a bit of breakfast?"

"You want breakfast, do you?" she roared. "You'll *be* breakfast if you're not careful. My husband the Giant is even bigger and taller than I am. He loves to eat boys like you for breakfast! He likes them so much he has them for lunch and dinner, too!" She laughed so loudly Jack's ears hurt.

Then the Giant's wife looked down at poor little Jack and said, "Oh, all right, come into the kitchen, and I'll give you some sour milk and stale bread."

As Jack ate, the castle began to quake, shake, and shudder. The Giant was on his way home, thumping the ground with his great big feet.

"Boy, if you don't want to be eaten, go and hide somewhere," said the Giant's wife. "Now!"

Jack quickly leapt off the table and did as she bid.

"Good morning, husband. Come into the kitchen and eat your breakfast," said the wife. The Giant stomped in and, sniffing the air with his great big nose, roared:

"Fee Fee Fi Fi Fo Fo Fum!
I smell the blood of an
    Englishman.
Be he alive or be he dead,
I'll grind his bones to make
    my bread!"

"No, no, my dear," said the Giant's wife. "I think you are still smelling that rascal you ate yesterday. Sit down and eat your breakfast. I cooked you two cows, twelve chickens, and fifty pounds of potatoes. If you don't eat, you'll shrink."

(TRY TO FIND JACK.)

Jack watched from his hiding place as the Giant sat and ate his breakfast. When the Giant finished eating, he took out a sack filled with gold coins and began to count them.

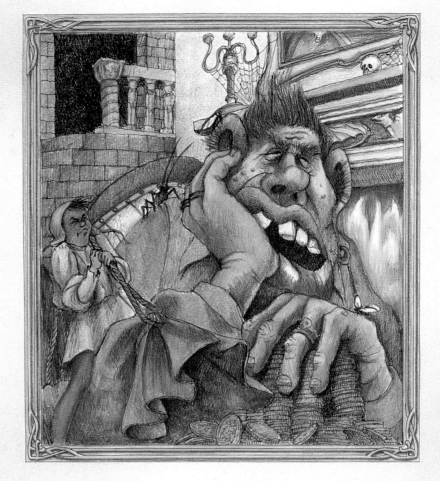

As he counted, he began to yawn and soon fell sound asleep. Quietly, Jack crept from his hiding place and tried to lift the sack of coins. The gold was much too heavy.

Jack had an idea.

He made a cart from buttons, knitting needles, and kitchen string. He heaved the sack of gold onto the cart and rolled it across the table.

Then Jack lowered the sack and the cart to the floor using a block and tackle he made from buttons, more string, needles, and two bones. Jack wheeled the gold to the beanstalk and dropped the sack down through the clouds to the ground below.

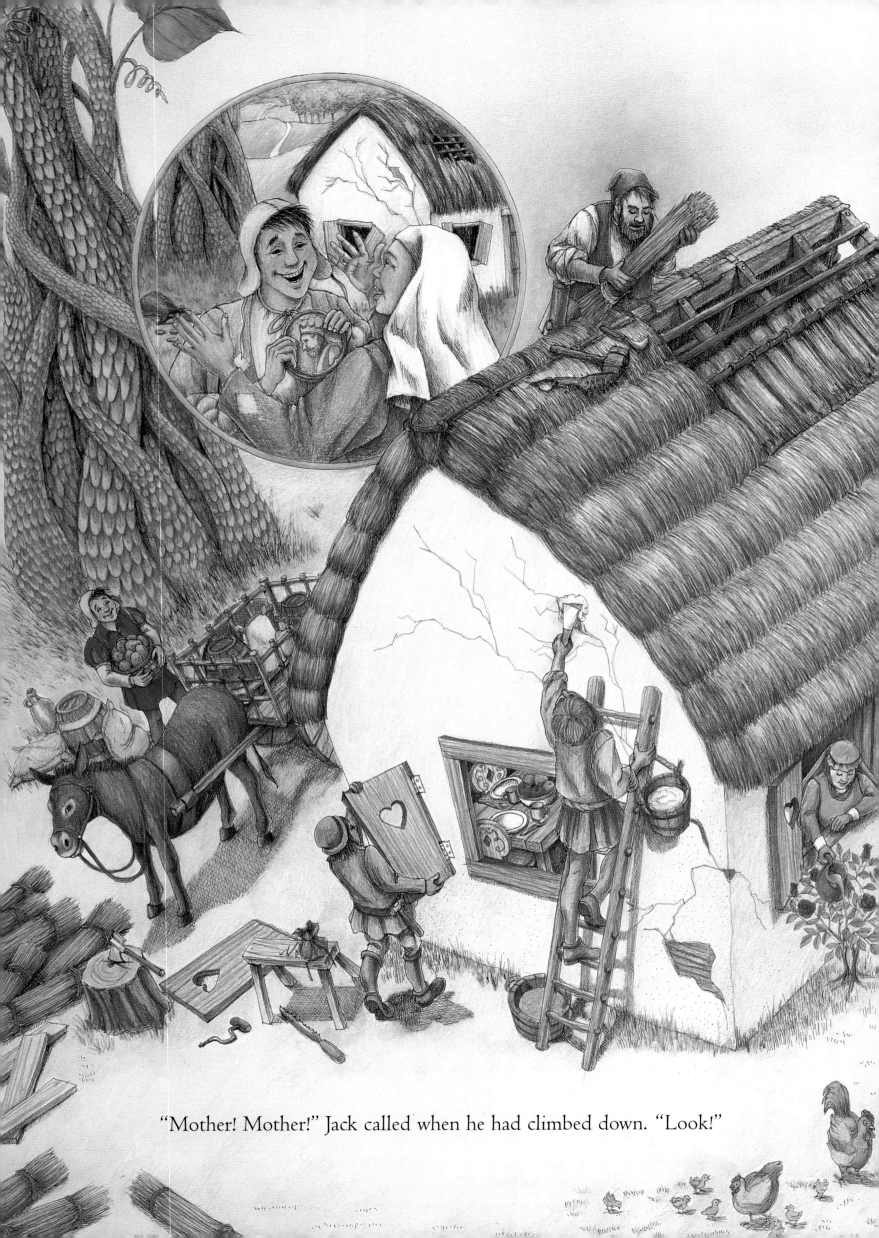

"Mother! Mother!" Jack called when he had climbed down. "Look!"

"Oh, my goodness! Now I can fill the cupboard with food," exclaimed Jack's mother.

"And we can buy some chairs to sit on, and some clothes, and a wagon, and coal for the fire," Jack added excitedly.

They lived frugally, but after a time the gold was spent. Jack decided to visit the Giant's castle again. This time he made sure he brought the proper equipment.

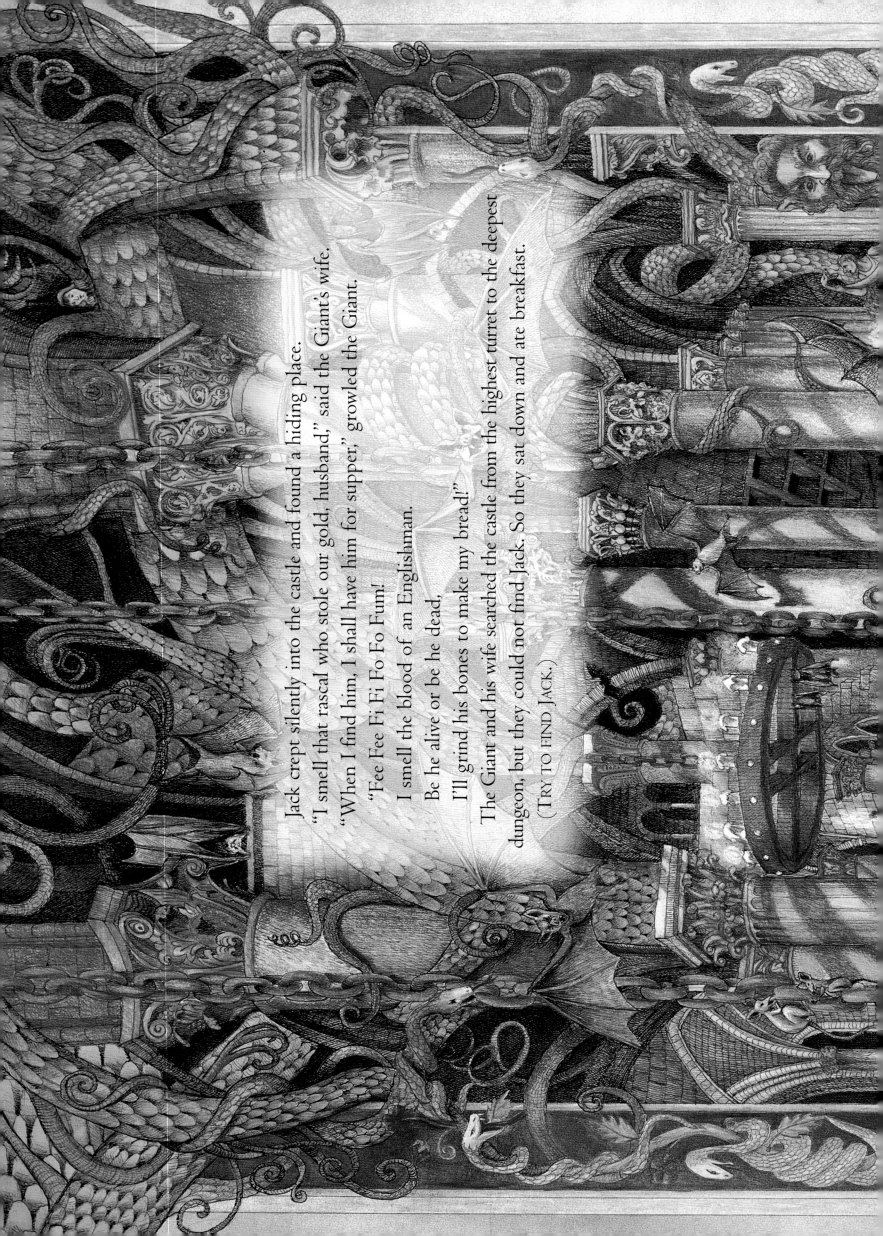

Jack crept silently into the castle and found a hiding place.

"I smell that rascal who stole our gold, husband," said the Giant's wife.

"When I find him, I shall have him for supper," growled the Giant.

"Fee Fee Fi Fi Fo Fo Fum!
I smell the blood of an Englishman.
Be he alive or be he dead,
I'll grind his bones to make my bread!"

The Giant and his wife searched the castle from the highest turret to the deepest dungeon, but they could not find Jack. So they sat down and ate breakfast.

(TRY TO FIND JACK.)

After they were through stuffing themselves, the Giant said to his wife, "Bring the hen that lays the golden eggs." When the hen was set in front of the him, the Giant commanded, "Lay!" The hen squawked and laid an egg of solid gold.

After so heavy a meal, the Giant and his wife soon fell asleep. Jack jumped from his hiding place. He took a napkin and made a hood to cover the hen's head so it would not be frightened. Jack then strapped the bird into the wife's sewing basket. He attached buttons to the basket for wheels and then lowered it to the floor. Jack rolled the basket to the beanstalk, lowered it to the ground, and then climbed down himself.

Jack and his mother were now very wealthy.

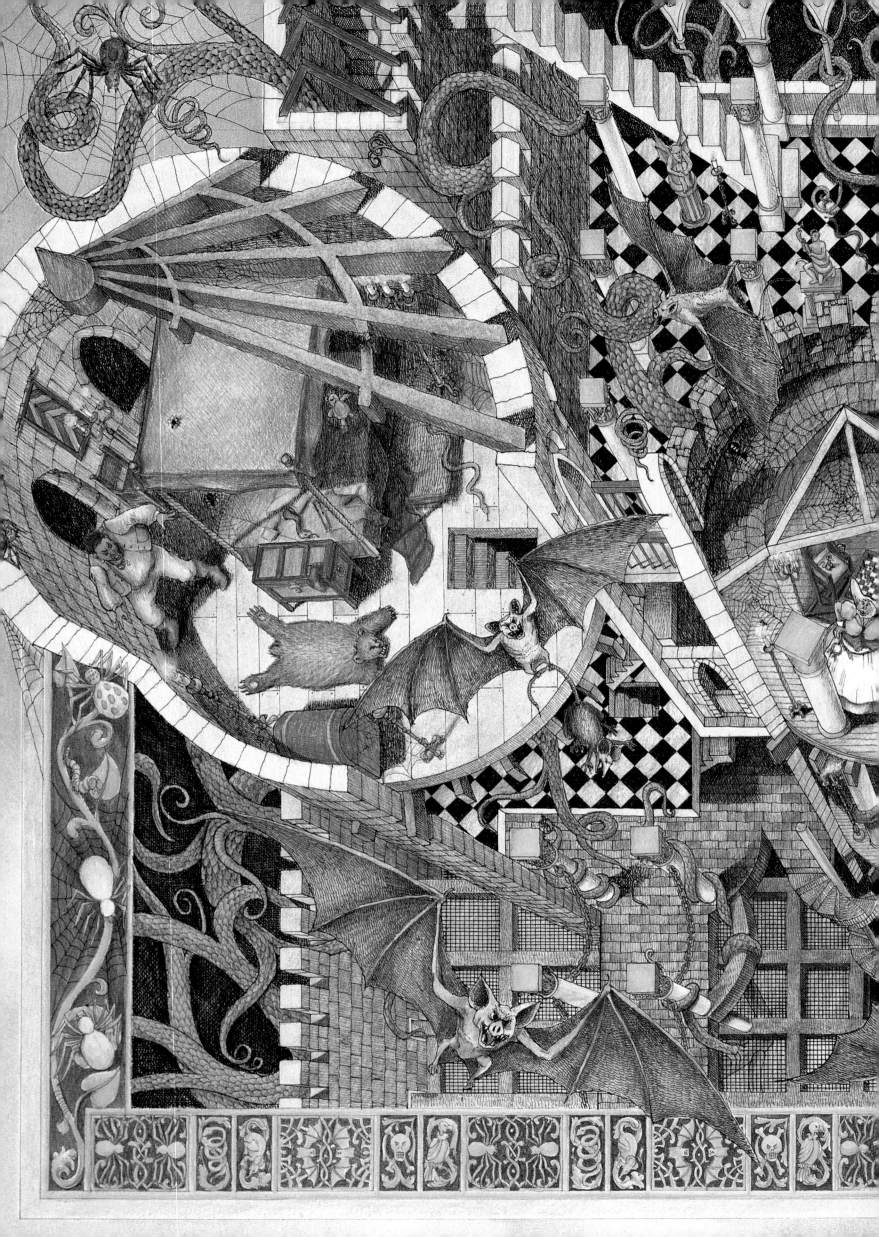

No matter how hard he tried, Jack could not
stop thinking about the Giant and his castle. He
decided to climb the beanstalk for a third time.
When he arrived at the castle, he hid once again.
The moment they smelled him, the Giant and his
wife roared together:
    "Fee Fee Fi Fi Fo Fo Fum!
    We smell the blood of an Englishman.
    Be he alive or be he dead,
    We'll grind his bones to make our bread!"

But they could not find Jack. (CAN YOU?)

After supper, the Giant called for his golden harp. The Giant slapped the table and commanded, "Sing, harp, sing!" The harp gently sang the Giant and his wife to sleep. Jack crept up behind the harp and signaled him to be quiet.

"I'll take you to a much more pleasant place to live," he said. The harp quickly agreed. Jack lashed buttons for wheels to the harp and pulled it toward the beanstalk.

On the way, Jack tripped and both he and the golden harp fell.

"Ouch!" the harp cried.

This commotion woke the Giant and his wife. They raced toward the sound and spied Jack just as he was lowering the harp to the ground. Jack scurried down the beanstalk with the Giant and his wife right behind.

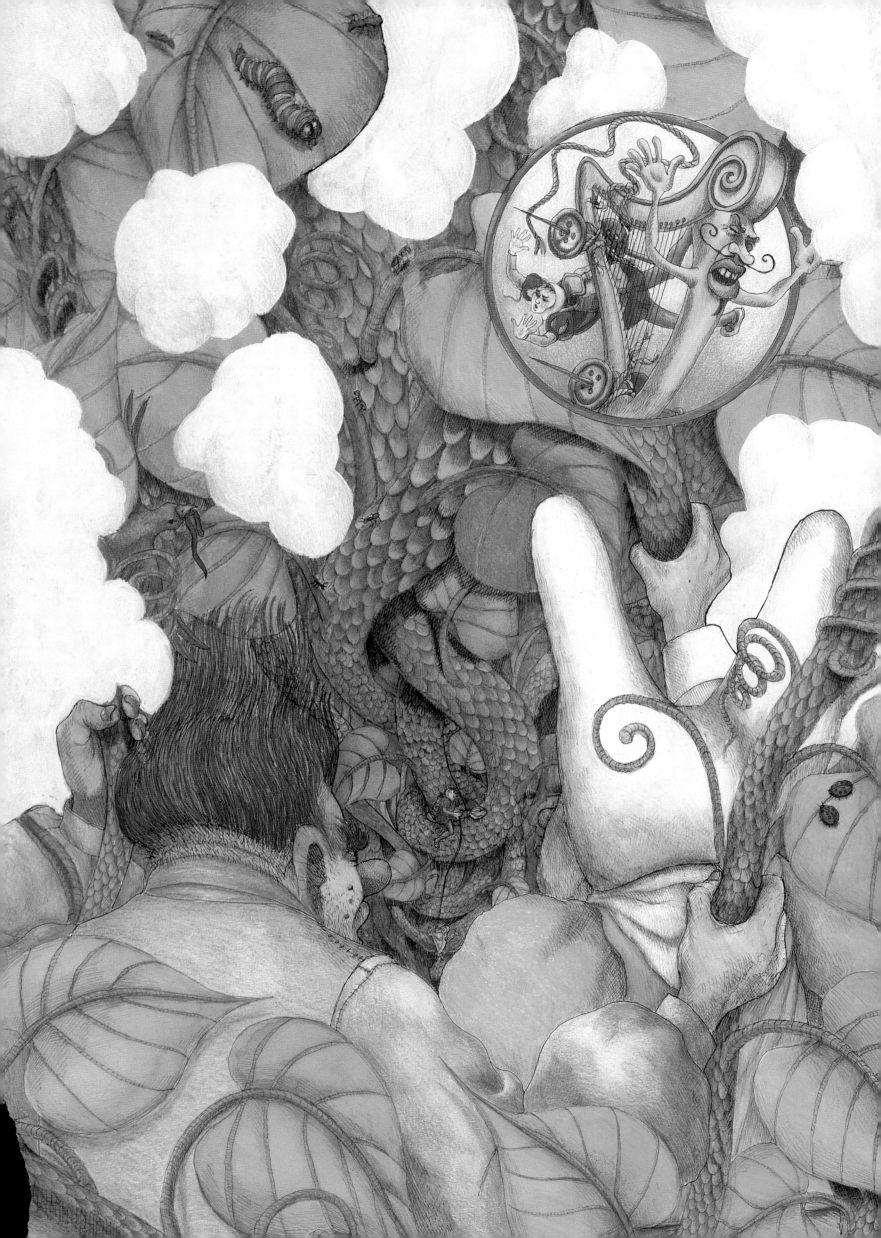

As soon as he reached the ground, Jack took an ax from his backpack and called,
"Mother, Mother! Come quick!"
Together they quickly chopped down the beanstalk.

With a thunderous crash, the beanstalk fell across the countryside into the sea. Both the Giant and his wife disappeared beneath the waves and were never seen again.

Jack and his mother shared their wealth with the entire town, and everyone lived happily ever after.

Author's Note

When I began this project, I read many versions of "Jack and the Beanstalk." Along with the picture books that I found at my local library and bookstore, I particularly found helpful the University of Southern Mississippi's Web site: "The Jack and the Beanstalk and Jack the Giant-Killer Project." It provided a wide range of retellings, beginning in 1820. From these various sources, I began to construct my own version.

I have always been fascinated with the proportions involved in the tale of Jack and his beanstalk. In the many versions that I read, the problem of scale was largely ignored. This bothered me. Fairy tales often ask us to suspend our disbelief. For example, we know giants don't really exist and that there are no beanstalks climbing to castles floating in the clouds. And we don't question how clouds can hold up a house of stone! But once the story's premise is accepted, then it must logically follow that the castle in which the Giant and his wife live is built to their proportions. So, defeating a fearsome Giant on his own territory will require a boy to be not only exceedingly brave but inventive as well.

SCALE: ONE SQUARE = ONE FOOT

FIGURE I

Using and exaggerating perspective helped me to dramatize the differences in scale. I have used plan perspective (looking down), section perspective (looking into), and worm's eye perspective (looking up) in order to dramatize Jack's adventures. I imagined the Giant to be about seventeen feet tall. Therefore Jack must figure a way to move through a castle where the seat of a chair is six feet above the ground, the top of a table is ten feet high, and each step of a staircase is two feet high. In addition, any other living creatures in the castle, be they pests or pets, are immense and threatening. Think of a cat as large as a Bengal tiger and just as hungry. (See figure I.)

My intent was to demonstrate the two important attributes Jack possesses: bravery and ingenuity. He must invent contraptions on the spot using materials on hand to overcome the Giant. It is this combination of courage

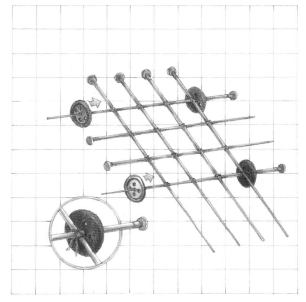

FIGURE 2

and the ability to think and improvise that makes Jack the small hero who wins the battle against the big Giant.

Jack transports the gold and the harp using a makeshift cart he constructs using buttons as wheels and knitting needles as axles. He uses strong string that the Giant's wife uses in her kitchen for rope to tie everything together. (See figure 2.)

Jack is able to lift the weight of the sack of gold and the hen with the aid of a homemade block and tackle. A pulley is a simple machine made up of a wheel and a rope. One end of the rope is attached to the load. The length of rope then fits on the groove of the wheel. When you pull on the rope's other end, the wheel turns and the load will move. Pulleys let you move loads up, down, or sideways. When two or more pulleys

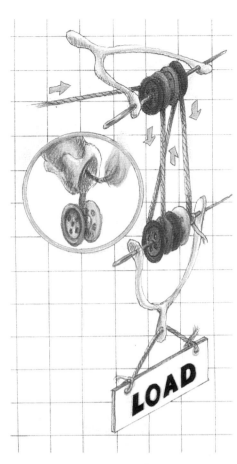

FIGURE 3

are connected and used together, they permit a heavy load to be lifted with less effort. This is called a block and tackle. Jack's pulleys were constructed by taking two buttons and attaching them with thread and wax to make a wheel. Bones and needles were added to create the block and tackle. (See figure 3.)

Joy Schleh and I begin each project the exact same way, with a phone call. We discuss our thoughts about the project, the kind of images we want to draw, the feeling each illustration should have. Then I usually fax Joy thumbnail sketches of how I see the work. We trade sketches and ideas and slowly refine the idea. As the drawings approach full scale, Joy helps me with clothing, lettering, fabric patterns, and border ideas. By this time we have a final pencil layout. I then usually take over and outline the layout in various colors of waterproof ink. I follow this by applying color, using color pencil, watercolor and airbrush until the piece is finished. Each final illustration is fifty percent larger than the printed one. All the illustrations are then photographed and scanned. I email the "final" work to Joy to get her comments. Each two-page spread took about sixty hours to complete from start to finish. The entire project took just over two years.

I tried to make the book a nonstop action adventure that builds to the explosive demise of the Giant, his wife, the beanstalk, et al. Although I was very happy to finish the project, it was also a sad moment. I will miss getting up in the morning and sitting at my drawing table. I will miss Jack and his endless adventures, and I will miss the mysterious beanstalk, the Giant, and his wife.

—A.L.

For "the girls": Maureen, Margaret, Kirsten

ACKNOWLEDGMENTS:

I would like to thank my daughter, Kirsten Guerin, for her creativity and skill; Neil Mahimtura for his professional assistance; my wife, Maureen, who was always ready with a clear point of view. Thanks are also due to my editor, Howard Reeves, for his insights, his guidance, and his patience; and to Emily Farbman and Becky Terhune for being real professionals.

Did you find Jack?

SPREAD 3 Jack is climbing the beanstalk. He is in the middle.

SPREAD 5 Jack is under the table next to the Giant's wife.

SPREAD 8 Jack is in the upper right-hand corner looking down.

SPREAD 10 Jack is behind the chair that a mouse is sitting on.

Designer: Sonia Chaghatzbanian
Illustrations are pen and ink, watercolor, and color pencil.

Library of Congress Cataloging-in-Publication Data

Lorenz, Albert, {date}
Jack and the beanstalk / retold by Al Lorenz.
p. cm.
Summary: A boy climbs to the top of a giant beanstalk, where he uses his
quick wits to outsmart an ogre and make his and his mother's fortune.
ISBN 0-8109-1160-4
[1. Fairy tales. 2. Giants—Folklore. 3. Folklore—England.] I. Title.

PZ8.L875 Jac 2002
398.2'0942'02—dc21
2001003751

Printed and bound in Hong Kong

10 9 8 7 6 5 4 3 2 1

 ▲ ABRAMS

Harry N. Abrams, Inc.
100 Fifth Avenue
New York, N.Y. 10011
www.abramsbooks.com

Abrams is a subsidiary of
 **LA MARTINIÈRE**
GROUPE